MAME YAA

THREE FRIENDS ADVENTUROUS JOURNEY

To order additional copies of this book, contact:
Xlibris
1-888-795-4274
www.Xlibris.com
Orders@Xlibris.com

I thank God for the success of this book.
Check out these other books "Little
Angelina" and "Woman who am I".

CHAPTER ONE

In a damp and sticky dark foggy forest lives an old lady in a little cottage who looks like she is older than her age yet had the strength of a young maiden; she is able to walk by herself yet she prefers to walk with a stick; she uses it as a guide during the night.

This forest is usually dark, gloomy and full of shady characters yet sometimes the sunlight spreads its light through and reveals its hidden softness. But this old lady is kind and fearless able to walk through the forest especially at night. Once as she was walking through the forest she came across a fox but she stood before the fox; said some unknown words and attempted to hit the fox with her walking stick and the fox disappeared. She has special powers to communicate with the forest therefore able to go through the forest as she pleases. She sometimes goes out in the night to communicate with some of the trees as sometimes they come to life as persons. Because of her special powers she was able to change her own surroundings into an admirable one. But her powers were only limited to her surroundings.

Every morning, the birds usually come to sing to her and convey messages which were mostly pleasant news. But this particular morning the sunlight that usually beamed across the forest did not show its face leaving the forest to be unusually dark; a strong wind blew through the forest pulling down strong and tall trees, small trees slamming and crashing against each other like drum sticks in the hands of a giant. All the animals went into hiding making the forest unusually quiet causing it to be creepier than usual. This strong rushing wind which has been destroying everything that stands in its way suddenly stopped and the forest became utterly quiet, no leaf dared move, the fluttering of wings was heard and the old lady came out from the cottage to meet them and enquired from them what the matter was. Tell me old friends what message you have for me.

Well our old friend, the birds said, listen to us very carefully, you know we travel from far and near therefore we have lots of information at hand. Hear what we have to say and you would know what is about to happen to us.

Go on I am listening, the old lady replied. You know I have always listened to what you have to say.

There are three friends who have decided to come to this forest to seek our hidden treasure but all three are of different character and understanding.

The first is Gred, he is greedy, doesn't listen to anything he is told, he takes what does not belong to him and thinks all that glitters is gold and therefore must have whatever he desires and want.

The second is called Qik, he is too quick to listen to anything being told and mostly miss out the vital details of information.

The third is called Pati, he is very careful in his doings and actions, careful to listen and careful in his choices. This is the one to free us all.

You must deal with all three fairly.

CHAPTER TWO

The sun light was fading, creating new shadows and dark patches as they approached the forest. Eyes curiously moving from tree hollows to fallen trees; the muddy sand gave its signature on their clothes and legs. The wind blew between slanted trunks, carrying the stink of rotten wood and earthy smell. Night time was fast approaching and they had just gotten into the forest. From a distance they thought they had seen a shadow.

Gred, mm.., did you see that? See what? That thing, what thing? The thing that just passed by. Qik asked impatiently; pointing his finger towards a cavy tree. Pati gave him a quick stare, warning him to keep quiet for fear that whatever it was might still be watching them.

Suddenly, they heard the sound as of a closing door and each turned at the direction of the sound then they realized the forest had changed from its original setting from what they saw as they walked in. a bitter chill passed through them and they began to hasten their steps walking through the dark forest seeking for a way out but the forest seemed never to end as they walked through in circles and always ended up where they started. They felt tired and decided to sit on an abandoned stone which was fastened to the ground. The shadow-like thing hid behind the dark shadows of the trees, they stood still watching the glow of red eyes carefully watching them; fright filled their eyes; their hearts began to beat faster than normal; one of them said in a whisper run yet they couldn't, all they could do were to walk backwards with their eyes fixed on the shadow. The shadow-like thing sensing their fear, lifted itself and flew up into the sky, what kind of a weird bird is this; another said. They run as fast as they could to hide from this creature in case it came back for them, this time they knew were dead.

Gred tiredly spoke; Pati...mm... he responded, can we rest for a while, he asked, as dawn was fast approaching, they felt tired to the core. Let's lie under one of those trees perhaps at sun rise we would know where we are and find a way out.

At last they found a tree which all could share, each sat next to the other feeling their warm skin and their warm breath which gave them a little warmth until sleep held its toes on them. They slept soundly but not for long, the groaning sounds of the trees woke them up. The dried leaves rustled under their feet as they rose up and moved back to see where the noise were coming from.

They were a bit startled for the moment but it soon died out. Noticing some fruits on the baobab tree, their stomach began to growl loudly reminding them of the emptiness it felt. Gred reached out his hand to take some of the fruits, Pati shouted, wait! The word had barely come out of his mouth when a rusty loud voice spoke, so loud the grounds they stood on began to shake.

Why have you come to disturb my sweet slumber and why do you have what is mine in your hands? The roots shot up and grabbed Qik wrapping itself around him tightly since he was closer. Gred on seeing this began to run but he barely got far, a branch swept him from the ground and wrapped itself around his legs and lifted him upside down with his head facing the ground. Pati could barely move and the same thing happened to him.

Thinking they were going to die, Qik managed to shout with a choking breath, do something or else we all die. Who is going to die? Gred asked rhetorically, yet with a stern rudeness in his voice. Angering the tree, it swirled its branches around spinning them until they began to beg for mercy and it stopped. Pati quickly cut in, we are sorry for the disturbance we have caused you, we didn't mean to take what belonged to you we were hungry and therefore took your fruits to satisfy our hunger. We are very sorry to have bothered you. At these words the tree loosened its grips and released them. They fell to the ground and scratched themselves against the rough bark of the roots they run as fast as their legs could take them.

Pati muttered thank you under his breath as he run on with the others.

CHAPTER THREE

Hush; said Gred, I can hear the sound of running water, his loud whisper cut through the air causing the others to be attentive to the wind which carried the scent of water and fresh trees along with it feeling their nostrils with freshness.

Hey! Look, wild berries Qik shouted. He rushed towards it and Gred followed, Pati warned, be careful you don't get swallowed up this time. Gred picked up a big twig and threw it against the plant waiting to see if there would be any reaction. Sure of their surroundings this time, they all rushed towards the berries and ate to their feel. The bees hummed in and out of the berry bushes as that was where they got their food to make their wild honey.

Since we don't know what is ahead of us, let's rest here for a day before we continue this perilous journey. They all agreed with Pati and rested until the sun began to set.

At the evening, when the sun was about to set but had not yet, the spread of its goldenness filled the whole forest creating a beautiful scenery and giving a beautiful touch to the forest the greener part of the leaves had the sun rays falling on them and therefore enriching that part of forest with a touch of gold

The shaft of light that hit the ground revealed the hidden softness that is only seen around this time of the day. The birds were flying and hopping from one tree to the other, while the deer run to take cover from their predators, and squirrels climbing trees for their pleasure. The grass at a distance felt soft and inviting.

They laughed their hearts out when a bird's nest containing bird's droppings instead of eggs fell upon Gred and splashed all over his faced.

The moon light touched their faces and a cool breeze slipped through the leaves across where they were lying. Heaviness fell upon them seeing the glow of animal eyes fixed on them they got up immediately and looked about themselves holding each other as a means of defense Pati picked a stick that was lying idly beside him and waved hard at it and it left.

CHAPTER FOUR

They worked their way along the narrow path, leaves gliding across their skins; they heard burble of water flowing over rock in a nearby stream. Moving faster, they felt they were close to the water but the more they walked the more the sound went farther. Wait I stepped on something, what is it this time, asked Gred impatiently. Qik.... Qik, Pati rushed over to him, Qik held his right foot up, I can't move he shouted. Pati bent over and took his left foot in his hands, he felt something dripped unto his hand by the touch of it he knew it was blood he kept it to himself being careful not to raise any panic. Gred growing impatient knelt to feel what has held his friend's foot fast to the ground. It was utterly dark this time, the thick leaves and trees were so thick and dense preventing the moonlight from reaching the ground; he couldn't see what it was, he felt it with his hand the first time but couldn't figure it out, at the second time; he knew what it was. Something hard stuck in it, he felt confused as he didn't know what to do to help him. A large root had staked its way around his other leg gripping it tightly and choking the life out of the leg, are you ok, he asked. His voice filled with immense concern.

The pain had become intense, all Qik could do was to cry; help guys he screamed, do something quickly I can't feel my legs anymore.

Pati grabbed the stick he had been holding, broke it into two to give it a sharpness, he quickly pierced the root out of instinct and quickly the roots loosed its hold and crawled away. Qik felt a bit of relieve, except for the stuck thing in his foot. Gred carried him on his back since he couldn't walk on the other foot. They walked on until finally they came across a large river. It was still dark and they didn't know how big and deep it was, they lied down in a grass nearby placing Qik carefully on the ground so not to cause him more pain than he already felt. They chatted and comforted themselves until they finally fell asleep while wondering how they would cross the river.

Who are you? Pati asked. A man stood before him; don't be afraid, he said. Afraid! Aha! He laughed aloud, what can make me afraid after all that we have gone through. I don't think anything can scare me anymore. Well son I came to tell you how you can cross the river, Pati suddenly felt his senses alert eager to listen to what he had to say. There is a hidden trumpet in those bushes across you, draw near and whistle three times the bushes will open and you will find a golden trumpet, pick it up and blow it twice a boat will come to you. You must first thank the skipper and then sit in it, but I warn you, no one must make noise otherwise you will drown; do well to remember what I have told you. He said this and vanished. Pati suddenly woke up at the sound of the birds and realized it was already morning. He narrated his dream to the others and hesitated no more but went to the bushes, whistled thrice, and indeed he found the trumpet and blew it twice, the water began to rattle and splash and a large old boat suddenly appeared on the water drawing closer to them. Just as the man had said they thanked the skipper and sat in the boat. They were all quiet until they reached the other side of the forest, Qik who was not able to bear the pain anymore gave a painful cry, the skipper, the boat and Qik vanished into the river leaving the two at the river bank.

Every time I think of these unexpected happenings it makes me feel nauseous; Gred said this with a bitter feel in his voice. They continued without knowing where they were going, at this time they had completely forgotten about finding the treasure they came to seek for. They were only trying to find a way out of the forest now. They had just realized they've been in the forest for three days and just about to start the fourth day.

CHAPTER FIVE

Deep in the forest, they walked without saying a word to each other. Each drowned in his own thoughts. Pati kicked some dried leaves, Gred felt in his face spider web strands, he cleared it from his face and cursed under his breath. A twig snagged from a tree and broke the intense silence between them.

Scratching his head, Gred asked, are you hungry? Pati looked at him for a while and smiled without saying a word but thought to himself; what kind of stupid question is this.

They walked on until from a distance they could see something that looked like a cottage. A bit of relief smiled upon their hearts as they thought they have a place finally to rest.

Sooner had they reached it than they thought they would. It was about sunset; the air was subtle; the trees utterly calm, blowing its leaves freely as the wind directed it.

Where is the door to this cottage? Gred asked walking around it. I don't think there is any, replied Pati. Now, what! Gred chuckled in an attempt to calm himself from his despair, he stamped his foot hard to the ground and then a door opened. Standing there astonished; both looked to each other's face and entered. They found two bowls filled with soup sitting on a table and two chairs beside it. They went in further and came across two neatly prepared beds with no one in it. It is as though someone was expecting us, Gred said. Pati shrugged, I'm just shocked as you. But becareful, don't touch anything, it may be a trap.

But Gred, usually not the type to listen, paid no heed to his advice; rushed into the chair, ate the bowl of soup to his fill and went straight to bed.

He began to feel strange movements in his stomach and yet he couldn't move out of the bed, the pain increased as every minute passed by. Pati tried with all his strength to get him out of bed but to no avail. Gred screamed for help but suddenly stopped, remaining silent thinking of what would happen to him.

Pati's eye brown creased as he was thinking about the current situation and what his last resort was going to be.

Suddenly, the door burst open, which made him jump from his bending position, relief flooded through him to see an old matured woman standing by the door.

Strangers, what are you doing in my house? She asked; saying it with such sarcasm, knowing that she was expecting them.

What! This is your house? Gred asked angrily. What kind of absurd house is this, look at me the trap you set has got me are you happy now.

Why should you talk to me with that harsh tone, I knew you were the disrespectful one? The old woman replied.

She made an attempt to hit him with her stick, but Pati quickly cut in. we deserve everything that has happened to us, at his word the woman turned to his direction, her anger melting away. What did you say? She asked. We are sorry for intruding into your privacy. We have come from a very far place seeking for treasure. So many misfortunes have we come across since we entered this forest, we finally thought we have found a place to rest our heads and then this happened to us please have mercy on us. As soon as she heard Pati's courteous speech she gave him a warm smile and said something unknown to them, Gred finally felt the pain subside and able to move from the bed.

CHAPTER SIX

The old lady hurried off to prepare food for them. They ate quietly until the woman broke into their silence.

What were your names again, she asked clearing her throat as though that would increase the volume of her words.

Well, we never gave it, said Gred still angry at her for what happened to him. She gave him a stern stare and shifted her attention to Pati.

Pati replied; I am Pati and my friend her is Gred. Yeah... that reminds me, you said earlier on that you knew my friend here was the rude one, how do you know us.

The old lady looked at Pati for a while and gave him a wry smile, my boy, she said; there is nothing hidden from me. I know why you are here and how you lost your other friend Qik. As soon as she mentioned Qik's name, they felt their hearts beating faster than usual and began to wonder who this woman was.

Calm down, she said worriedly, in an attempt to calm their hearts down, knowing how uneasy each felt.

You can rest in my cottage two nights and then continue your journey. No harm will come to you here. They gave a sigh of relief and heeded to her advice.

Pati's eyes were heavy as a sand bag and could not wait any longer therefore headed to one of the beds and slept in. it felt comfortable soon he felt into a deep sleep.

Gred on the other hand hesitated to sleep in the other bed for the fear of his previous incident and therefore laid beside Pati on his bed. They finally had a good sleep for the first time.

The chattering of the birds woke them up from the good sleep they have had for the first time since they entered the forest. The birds came to give their usual greetings since it was morning. The old lady came to chat with the birds and left for her usual duties in the forest.

Pati looked up at the beautiful pattern of the blue sky which the long leaves from the tall and slender trees had created and allowed the sunlight to dance across his face. It felt warm and for the first time in their journey he felt at home. He was amazed at how the birds danced in circles and approached him without fear.

Gred on the other hand threw stones at some lizards and squirrels that were climbing up and down of trees. For a moment he starred at a particular place something had caught his attention. He walked towards it and looked at it for a while, he bent over and picked it up, realizing it was a precious ruby, he put it in his pocket and walked away as though nothing had happened.

Pati noticed a change in his appearance and mood; is something wrong, he asked?

No, he replied; when are we leaving I think we have already wasted much time; we have to get going. Pati watched him as he walked to the cottage, he noticed something awkward about him but couldn't place his hands on it. He shook his head and ignored him and then focused his attention on the birds and the beautiful surroundings he was standing in.

Wake up, wake up…. O…o….ooo! What is it Gred? Its dawn we have to leave. Ok, he responded sleepily. As they prepared to leave, the old lady warned them to be careful on the road.

Be careful, she warned; for as you get deeper into the forest, the more pleasant the things look. In fact, it looks inviting and pleasant to the eye but none of them are real. In actual fact the bigger things are not real, pick only small things that look unpleasant to the eye.

CHAPTER SEVEN

They set out into the forest to seek the treasure as they realized they were closer to it than ever. As they walked deeper into the forest they began to realize that everything they were told were true; in fact, it was more pleasing to the eye than how they heard it; it was indeed breath taking at the sight of it. The forest shined with a pleasant glow which made it very attractive. Insects of different kinds and sizes flew around colorfully. Fruits were large and could be eaten for weeks by an entire village. A fresh organic smell filled the forest making it quite soothing to the heart. You could taste the sweetness of the fruits by the scent of it. What made it intriguing were the pearls and rubies that were stuck on them.

Gred seeing this ignored the old lady's advice and tried to pick them but Pati called out to him from behind to stop. They walked further on, this time Gred couldn't contain the pleasure he was feeling at the sight of the pearls. He thought to himself; why pay attention to some stupid old woman's advice while I can make plenty of money from these precious stones. He couldn't bear his greed anymore; he started picking them from the fruits. A large fruit which had the ability to talk and was quite tempting whispered into his ears; pick me up and I will make you rich forever. As soon as he heard this he smiled to himself and picked the fruit, he had barely touched it when he vanished into thin air leaving Pati all by himself.

Pati also heard a loud whisper from another tempting fruit and he ignored it and yet again another but this time an unpleasant skinny looking fruit that had watery bruises on it; don't pick me up for I am unpleasant to be held; it said. He rushed unto it and took it and he heard something sighing and saying thank you for considering me. The earth shook and suddenly, a door appeared and opened before him.

He entered into a room which was immensely dark that he could feel the touch of it on his body. He couldn't see anything about him except the feel of the grounds he was standing on. Reaching out his hands he felt the walls around him and then he touched something, it felt like a switch, he pressed it hard, the room became slightly brightened as the switch was an archaic invention that someone was trying to do.

He looked around the room carefully but he didn't see any treasure except some long stairs that could take thousand years to climb. He felt disappointed that he had come a long way for nothing yet he felt the need to press on.

He took his first step then he realized the stairs were not longer and many but has become few in his eyes. Yet he took another step again and the stairs became less, he finally climbed the last one and there were no more stairs to be seen. He walked into a vast room that had it doors opened; a colorful large curtain which had small intricate floral embroideries sewn into it draped gorgeously on the marbled floor and this was all he could see. He moved on to two other rooms with hopes of finding the treasure but he discovered something; neither of the rooms had any treasure in them except this room which had two large golden thrones which were fastened to the ground such that at the sight of it; it is as though it was carved from the ground in one piece. He heard the echoes of his footsteps as he walked in, sometimes he turned to see if he was being followed. The air had a rusty dusty smell in it which made him cough the first time he inhaled it when he entered this room.

The thrones had not been used in years and so had dust and cobwebs covering all over. He wiped some dust away from the king's throne which was the largest one; he sat on it to at least give him the pleasure of sitting on a golden throne and take some of the disappointments away. Little did he know he was the key to the breaking away of the curse the forest was under and by sitting on the king's throne was the key to undo this curse.

CHAPTER EIGHT

A sudden strong wind filled the room and whirled itself in the center for a while and then stopped. A bright light glowed in the room; he saw two creatures descending from the sky through an open window which had large patterns of dusty square panels; the crescent moon in the sky made it look as though they were coming from the moon. As they came closer he became terrified, quickly he hid himself behind the throne for fear of them finding him.

As soon as their feet touched the floor the whole place changed from its rustiness and unpleasant sight to a magnificent and splendid room; the intricate patterns and arrangement of the marbles was a sight to behold; the throne had four golden eagles in front of it; three on each side. The stairs of the thrones had large floral relief patterns carved in it and therefore complimenting the throne with an impressive sight.

They went to sit on their thrones respectively; a light went forth from them and entered the forest a thick large blanket of dark clouds lifted itself off the forest giving way to the light. Everything came back to its normal state.

The baobab tree became a man and went about the king's duties as the king's advisor; the fruits became the towns' men and women and also went about their normal duties. The cottage became a magnificent building and the old lady became a beautiful maiden who was the king's daughter therefore the princess of the town. The birds that usually sang to the old lady were the children of the town and they also went to their respective homes.

The whole town was filled with joy and celebrations.

CHAPTER NINE

Pati on seeing how the two people approached and sat on the throne and when no harm had come to him came out of his hiding place with a bit of fright in him.

Hesitating to approach the king, the king bid him to come closer and gave him a warm smile. A beautiful maiden appeared; her presence brought warmth to the palace. As soon as her eyes met Pati's, her heart was filled with love towards him and his towards her. She gave her dad a warm embrace and sat beside her mother full of smiles.

I know your mind is wandering and seeking for answers I will tell you all about it.

A long time ago, peace and harmony reigned in this town everyone gave love to each other in everything they did and said. Until one day a stranger who was envious of us came and dwelt among us. He started brain washing our men and women with bad advice and they began to develop greed, hatred for one another and impatience began to rule our peoples' hearts; people started taking what did not belong to them, they grew impatient toward one another and hatred ruled their hearts. When the stranger saw that he had succeeded in his mission he placed a curse on the town and turned it into a hideous forest so that no one would be able to save it.

Finally, he said until we have learnt the lesson of patience, love, and showed no greed towards each other and moreover until the one person who possessed all these three qualities come into the forest and share the king's power by sitting on the king's throne, the forest would continue to be under the curse. We had hope when we heard his last words but those who came to the forest did not possess these qualities and therefore failed until you came.

When Pati heard this he realized that it was not a treasure he came to seek but a destiny he came to fulfill.

Pati also narrated all that happened to him- and his friends and the king and queen listened with much attention; sometimes he paused and shed tears for his friends and continued to the last detail.

The king and queen assured him that everything was going to be all right.

The king continued; since this was the promise we made that anyone who freed us from this curse would have my daughter in marriage and rule the kingdom with me; now I have to fulfill that promise therefore I give my daughter to you as your wife. Tomorrow the ceremony would take place.

Early in the morning, the wedding ceremony began; the whole town was filled with nice scented flowers and in a joyous mood.

Pati; now a prince was dressed in the most magnificent robe which had its embroideries laid with gold and a beautiful crown was set on his head.

The princess had a gold and white linen gown adorned on her and a beautiful golden crown to compliment the dress. The whole town came as witnesses to the wedding; the celebrations lasted for a whole month.

Oh! By the way, Gred and Qik came back to life and all those who failed to free the forest.

And the lesson love, patient and being content with one another was learnt.

CPSIA information can be obtained at www.ICGtesting.com
Printed in the USA
BVIW12100215051 9
548350BV00009B/63

* 9 7 8 1 7 9 6 0 3 2 0 6 2 *